Change Sings

A
Children's
Anthem

Amanda Gorman   Loren Long

PUFFIN

I can hear change humming
In its loudest, proudest song.

I don't fear change coming,
And so I sing along.

I scream with the skies
Of red and blue streamers.

I dream with the cries
Of tried-and-true dreamers.

I'm a chant that rises and rings.

There is hope where my change sings.

Though some don't understand it,
Those windmills of mysteries,

I sing with all the planet,
And its hills of histories.

I hum with a hundred hearts,
Each of us lifting a hand.

I use my strengths and my smarts,
Take a knee to make a stand.

I'm bright as the light each day brings.

There is love where my change sings.

I show others tolerance,
Though it might take some courage.

I don't make a taller fence,

But fight to build a better bridge.

I talk not only of distances,

From where and how we came.

I also walk our differences,
To show we are the same.

I'm a movement that roars and springs,
There's a wave where my change sings.

Change sings where? There! Inside me.

Because I'm the change I want to see.

As I grow, it grows like seeds.

I am just what the world needs.

I'm the voice where freedom rings.
You're the love your bright heart brings.

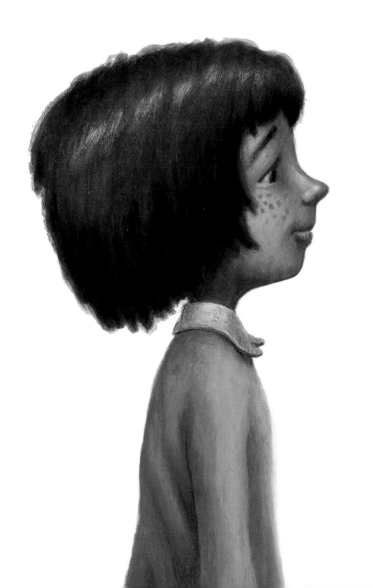

We are the wave starting to spring,
For we are the change we sing.

We're what the world is becoming,
And we know it won't be long.

We all hear change strumming.
Won't you sing along?

For my mom,
who always believed in my voice.
—AG

For Tracy,
who is always a vital part of my work.
—LL

PUFFIN BOOKS

UK | USA | Canada | Ireland | Australia
India | New Zealand | South Africa

Puffin Books is part of the Penguin Random House group of companies
whose addresses can be found at global.penguinrandomhouse.com.

www.penguin.co.uk   www.puffin.co.uk   www.ladybird.co.uk

Penguin
Random House
UK

First published in the USA by Viking, an imprint of Penguin Random House LLC, 2021
Published in Great Britain by Puffin Books, 2021

001

Text copyright © Amanda Gorman, 2021
Illustrations copyright © Loren Long, 2021

Design by Jim Hoover
Text set in Moranga and Grobek

The art for this book was created by hand on illustration board, using acrylics and coloured pencil

Printed and bound in China

The authorized representative in the EEA is Penguin Random House Ireland,
Morrison Chambers, 32 Nassau Street, Dublin D02 YH68

A CIP catalogue record for this book is available from the British Library

ISBN: 978–0–241–53583–7

The publisher does not have any control over and does not assume any responsibility
for author or third-party websites and their content.

All correspondence to:
Puffin Books
Penguin Random House Children's
One Embassy Gardens, 8 Viaduct Gardens, London SW11 7BW